I AM

AWESOME

Written by: Patricia Brioux
Illustrated by: Floyd Yamyamin

Tellwell Talent
www.tellwell.ca

ISBN
978-0-2288-4022-0 (Hardcover)
978-0-2288-4021-3 (Paperback)
978-0-2288-4023-7 (eBook)

Dedication

For Cole, Blake, Evy, Kurtis, Stella, Cam, Jocee, and Luke. You guys are ROCK STARS. Love you to the moon and back!
AND
For my sister-in-law Trace, "I showed up today, I am stronger today, AND I AM AWESOME!" (Tracey Brioux)

Special Thanks
Steph,
I have no words. Thanks for being the BEST aunt in the world!

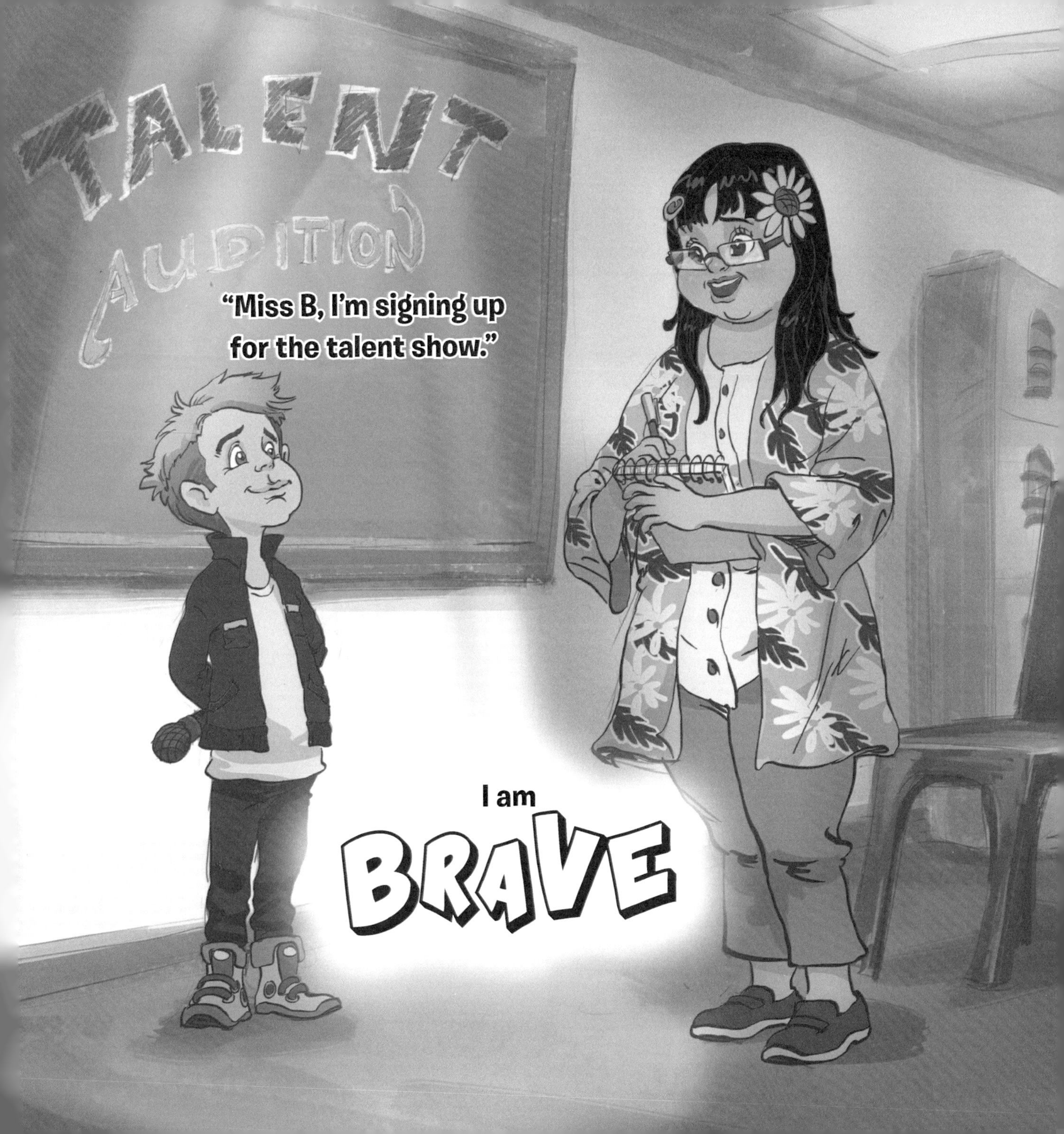

"Miss B, I'm signing up for the talent show."

I am

BRAVE

I am

SMART

"Sissy, watch. Me do it myself."

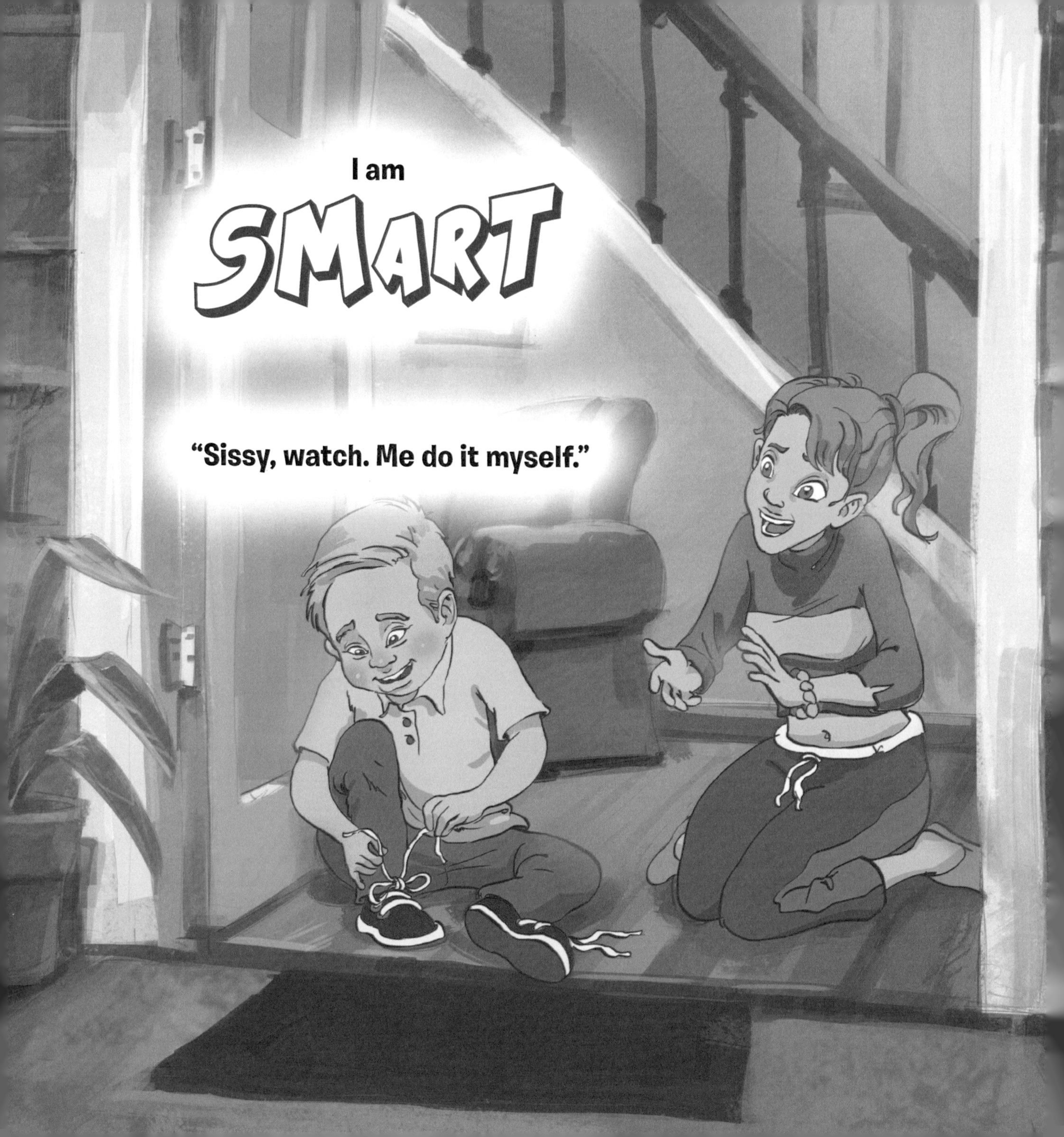

I am
POWERFUL

"I can do anything I
set my mind to."

I am HONEST

"I never ever ever lie."

"Me either."

"My mama says if you lie your nose will grow so, so, so big like Pinocchio and a wolf will cry and no one will ever believe you again."

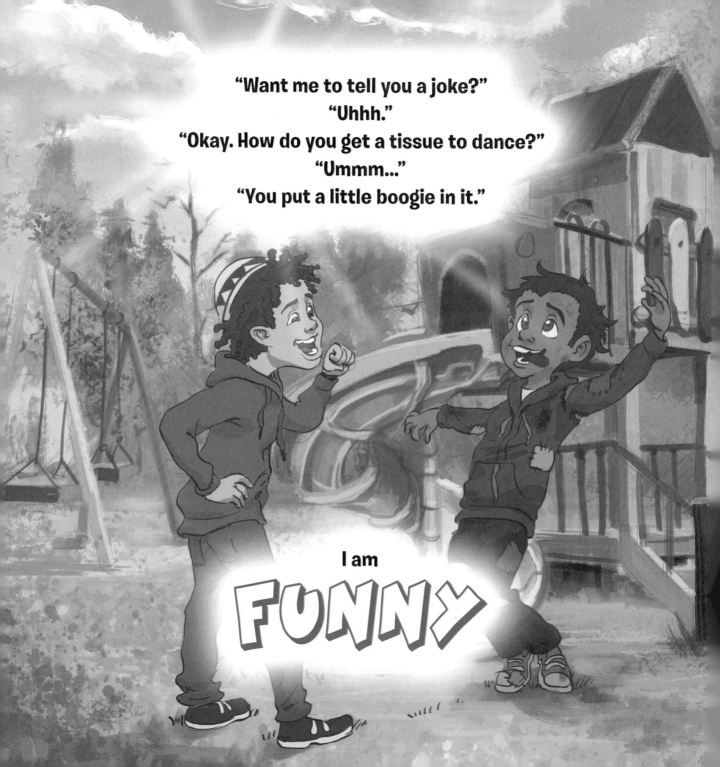

I am ME...

AND I AM AWESOME!

About the Author

Patricia Brioux is not a New York Times, Amazon Top 100, or a USA Today bestselling author but she is the daughter of two rock star parents, the youngest of six kids, and the FUN aunt to eight crazy little kiddos who just love to keep her on her toes. This is her first literary published work, and to be honest that both excites and terrifies the heck out of her. Through this process she hopes to learn, become more confident, and, who knows, maybe one day work alongside some of the greats like Nora Roberts, Kennedy Ryan, and Kelly Elliott

CPSIA information can be obtained
at www.ICGtesting.com
Printed in the USA
LVRC101223160721
692764LV00006B/6

* 9 7 8 0 2 2 8 8 4 0 2 2 0 *